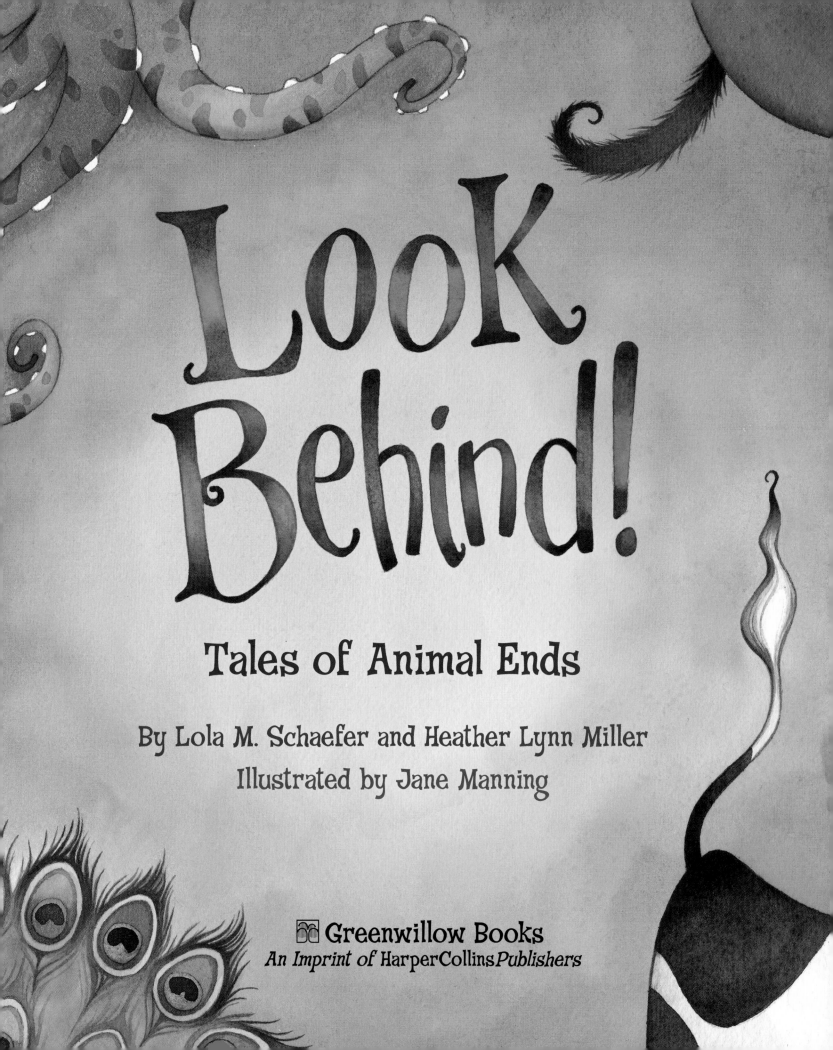

Look Behind!

Tales of Animal Ends

By Lola M. Schaefer and Heather Lynn Miller

Illustrated by Jane Manning

Greenwillow Books
An Imprint of HarperCollinsPublishers

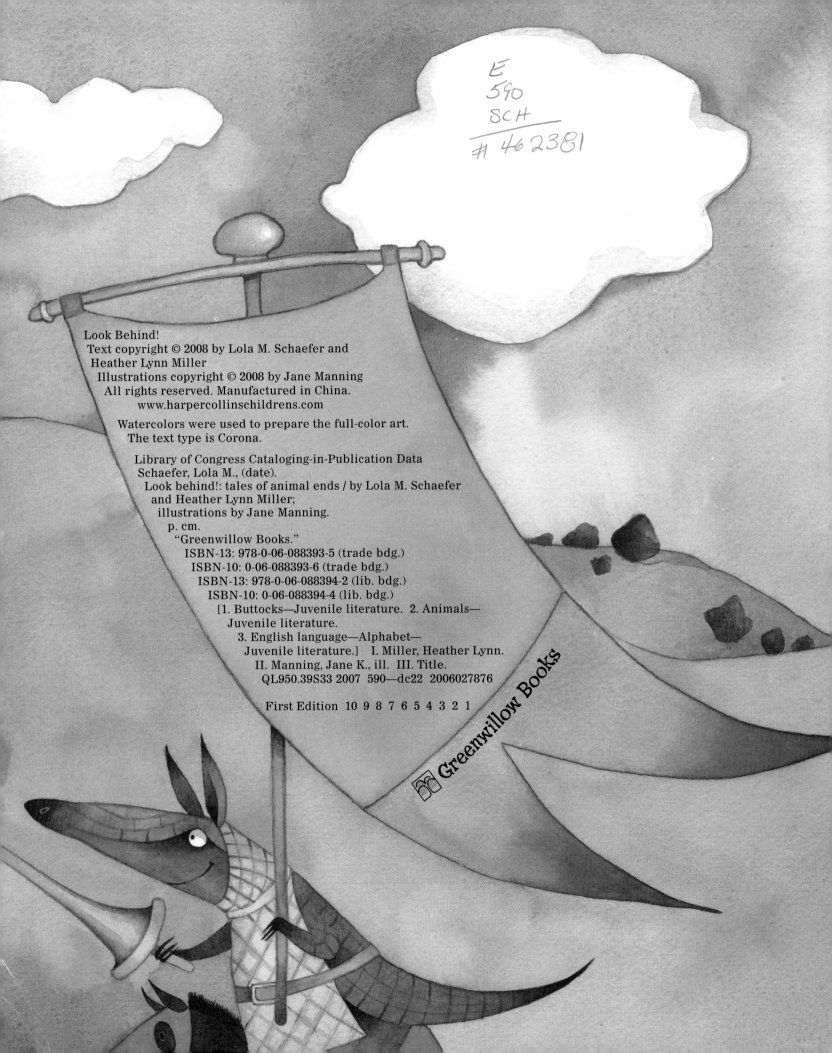

Look Behind!
Text copyright © 2008 by Lola M. Schaefer and
Heather Lynn Miller
Illustrations copyright © 2008 by Jane Manning
All rights reserved. Manufactured in China.
www.harpercollinschildrens.com

Watercolors were used to prepare the full-color art.
The text type is Corona.

Library of Congress Cataloging-in-Publication Data
Schaefer, Lola M., (date).
Look behind!: tales of animal ends / by Lola M. Schaefer
and Heather Lynn Miller;
illustrations by Jane Manning.
p. cm.
"Greenwillow Books."
ISBN-13: 978-0-06-088393-5 (trade bdg.)
ISBN-10: 0-06-088393-6 (trade bdg.)
ISBN-13: 978-0-06-088394-2 (lib. bdg.)
ISBN-10: 0-06-088394-4 (lib. bdg.)
[1. Buttocks—Juvenile literature. 2. Animals—
Juvenile literature.
3. English language—Alphabet—
Juvenile literature.]   I. Miller, Heather Lynn.
II. Manning, Jane K., ill. III. Title.
QL950.39S33 2007 590—dc22 2006027876

First Edition 10 9 8 7 6 5 4 3 2 1

Greenwillow Books

For Madeline,
whose curious thoughts
led us to the end
—L.M.S. and H.L.M.

To Natalie and Darby,
with love
—J.M.

Did you know that animal butts are amazing?

They are!

Just like you, animals use their rear ends

to stand, walk, bend, and sit.

But some animal rumps do so much more.

They scare enemies,

light the night,

or even disappear before your eyes.

Turn the page to learn the scoop behind . . .

animal butts.

B

Imagine ice skating in your underwear! The walrus plays on the ice in its bare skin every day. Like a cozy winter coat, a thick layer of fat called *blubber* helps keep the walrus, and its rump, warm as it swims through the icy-cold waters. A male walrus is insulated by so much heavy blubber that it must use its tusks to help drag itself onto shore.

Crusty Butt

A horseshoe crab wears its bones on the outside of its body. Sound weird? It's not! The shell, called an *exoskeleton*, protects the animal and gives it its trademark shape. It also makes the animal feel crusty to the touch, even on its bottom.

Blubber Butt

Dirty Butt

A warthog likes to wallow, or roll, in muddy streams and lakes. When the mud dries, it protects the warthog. Biting flies and other insects cannot reach the warthog's skin, especially its hind end. The mud also hides the skin from the heat of the sun. *Aaaaah*, there's nothing like a good mud bath.

Electric Butt

An electric fish uses special cells to make electrical charges. This electricity guides the fish through muddy river water. It can also stun enemies, kill prey, or send electrical messages to other fish. Any animal that bites an electric fish on the back end will be in for a shocking surprise!

F Fancy Butt

It's showtime! The peacock steals the stage with his fabulously fancy fanny.
As his act begins, the peacock struts about, searching for a female. Then, in one
swift movement, he spreads his fan of brilliantly colored tail feathers. Finally,
with a crazy wiggle of his rump, the peacock sends his feathers shakin' and
quakin', makin' the females go wild. Bravo, Mr. Peacock!

G
Glowing Butt

Fireflies flash their lighted rear ends to let one another know where they are. But how do they do it? It's a lot like glow-in-the-dark light sticks, which make light by mixing two chemicals together. Fireflies mix similar chemicals inside their bodies to make their rear ends glow. It's quick. It's simple. It's *chemiluminescence*!

Hairy Butt

Taking a dip in freezing water may sound chilling to you, but the polar bear doesn't mind at all. Two layers of thick hair keep this Arctic animal warm from head to hind end. Although the polar bear's fur looks white, each hair is actually clear. This lack of color helps the polar bear hide on the snow and ice.

Invisible Butt

Now you see it, now you don't! A walking stick is a brown-and-green insect that is long and thin. Its shape and markings make it look like the plants it eats. This camouflage hides the insect from hungry enemies.

Juicy Butt J

A salamander, like all amphibians, is moist to the touch. Glands make sticky mucus that prevents the animal's skin from drying out. This salamander also has glands that manufacture a wet poison. The salamander's bottom looks extra juicy, but the poison tastes bad and can make the animal's enemies sick. So, if you see a bright salamander, look . . . but don't touch!

Knight in Shining

Prepare to battle! An armadillo is always ready—to protect itself. Its body is covered with bands of bony plates. The plates are capped with horns. If an animal comes from behind and bites an armadillo on the rump, it will get a mouthful of crackle and crunch!

Armor Butt

L

Lumpy L Butt

The male midwife toad carries a lumpy load. The female toad lays eggs in a string, like beads on a necklace. The male wraps the eggs around his legs and backside, where he carries them for several weeks. As the eggs hatch, the male lowers himself into a pond and sets the new tadpoles free.

Shorter than an earthworm and tinier than an ant, the mosquito is a mini-sized insect with a mini-sized butt. With a name that means "little fly," mosquitoes have been given a suitable title. Although the American gallinipper is a whopping one inch long, most mosquitoes are no larger than a sesame seed.

Every time a cow breaks wind, it releases methane gas into the air. Too much methane in the atmosphere can raise the earth's temperature. But the gas isn't always bad. Methane can be used to make electricity. Some farmers are experimenting with ways to capture methane. Maybe someday your television will be powered by the gas collected from a cow's noisy rear end!

Oil and water don't mix. In this case, that's a good thing! A duck spends most of its life in water, but it doesn't want wet, cold feathers. A gland under its tail makes oil. While preening, the duck uses its head and beak to spread this oil over and between all of its feathers. The oil waterproofs the feathers to keep the duck dry and warm.

Popping P Butt

The bombardier beetle is a living science lab. It makes two different chemicals inside its bottom. When the beetle is frightened, it mixes these two chemicals together. The mixture heats up until it almost boils. The beetle aims its bottom and . . . POP! POP! POP! The hot liquid bursts out and sprays the beetle's enemy. *Ouch!*

Quill

Eight, nine, ten . . . ready or not, here it comes! Imagine playing hide-and-seek with a creature that can change colors in the blink of an eye. Sound like something from outer space? Try under the sea. Many octopi are equipped with special skin cells filled with colored pigments. The octopus mixes the pigments to make hundreds of color changes each day.

Butt!

Beware! A porcupine's body is covered with hair and thousands of quills. Quills are stiff spines with hooks called *barbs* on their ends. To protect itself, a porcupine turns its rump toward an attacker. It rattles its quills as a warning. If that doesn't frighten the enemy away, a poke in the face will.

Rainbow Butt

Slimy

The hippo covers itself from head to hind end with its very own sunscreen.
Like sweat, sticky slime oozes up from tiny holes in the hippo's skin.

Butt

Chemicals in the slime absorb the sun's harmful rays and protect the
hippo's skin. But hippo slime isn't about to find its way into your beach
bag anytime soon. Hippo scientists say the slime is super stinky.

Tricky Butt

With a head that looks like an end and an end that looks like a head, the shingleback lizard can be quite confusing. That's the whole point. Hungry predators aren't sure which end to attack when they move in on the shingleback. Can you tell which end is which?

U

Upside-Down Butt

The sloth spends most of its life hanging around, upside down in trees. Using its long, long claws, this animal grips the tree branches high above the rain-forest floor, where it eats, sleeps, and gives birth upside down. The sloth crawls to the ground once every eight days and turns its rear end right side up to go to the bathroom.

Vampire Butt

Once a year or so, a hungry leech attaches to another animal. It bites the skin and sucks its blood. As the leech fills up, its body swells until it is three, four, or five times larger. Later the leech uses the blood as food, and its body shrinks back to its smaller size. Then it's ready for another good bite of blood.

Push! Wiggle! Wiggle! A worm has two groups of muscles. One group circles its body like rings. When these muscles tighten, the worm gets longer and pushes its front end forward. Another group of muscles runs from the front of the worm to the back, like long rubber bands. When these muscles tighten, the back end wiggles toward the front.

Extinct X Butt

This dinosaur's rump weighed almost 2,000 pounds and was as tall as a school bus. But don't worry, you two won't ever meet. Stegosaurus and all the other dinosaurs are extinct. They died millions of years ago. Even though you can't find a living dinosaur today, you can view a fossil of one from long, long ago.

Yoga Butt

Point those doggie duffs up toward the sky. It's yoga time! A dog uses its body to show how it feels. If the dog lies on its back, it may be frightened. Hanging its head may show that it's unhappy. If a dog wants to play, it lowers its head and shoots its wiggly rear end up toward the sky. *Ruff! Ruff! Ruff!*

Zany Butt

Z

With black-and-white stripes zipping this way and that, it's hard to tell one zebra from another. That's the idea! Zebras stand close together in groups called *herds*. They watch for danger while their zany stripes confuse hungry enemies. Over there—is that the head of a zebra? The back? The front? No, it's definitely . . .

THE END.